STARFISHERS to the Rescue

by
Ellen Dreyer

Illustrated by Drew-Brook-Cormack

Modern Curriculum Press
Parsippany, New Jersey

Cover and book design by Agatha Jaspon

Modern Curriculum Press
An imprint of Pearson Learning
299 Jefferson Road, P.O. Box 480
Parsippany, NJ 07054–0480

www.pearsonlearning.com

1-800-321-3106

ISBN 0-7652-0886-5

6 7 8 9 10 11 12 13   MA   07 06 05 04 03 02 01

CONTENTS

For Mom and Dad,
who also love the sea.

Chapter 1

A Home in the Sea

"Wait up!" Ana Ramirez called to Daniel Fisher and Laura Marks. The three were riding their underwater scubaboards near a coral reef. Daniel had spotted some dolphins playing nearby and sped off with Laura. Ana, who was looking at some angelfish, was left behind.

She took off after them, but the water was cloudy. She could not see where they had gone.

She thought about pressing the HOME button. The computer inside her scubaboard would then take her back to the Starfish.

The Starfish was a science research station. It sat on the bottom of the Pacific Ocean not far from the Hawaiian Islands. It was called the Starfish because it had been built with five arms around a center. It looked a lot like a starfish from above.

Several families had lived and worked on the Starfish since 2051. It was like a small town underwater. Seaweed and fish farms were nearby. Special machines changed saltwater into freshwater for drinking.

Ana's mother was a marine biologist. She wanted to study the coral reefs in the South Pacific. Ana herself loved the ocean. She had looked forward to working with dolphins.

Ana was finding it hard to get used to living in the Starfish. It was so different from living on the mainland. She was beginning to wonder if she would ever be a Starfisher. She had to remember that she had moved to the Starfish only two weeks ago.

Just then she felt a nudge at her elbow. A bottlenose dolphin bumped her playfully.

"Hey, stop that!" she said, laughing.

Through her helmet speaker, Ana heard the dolphin's sounds. Ana knew a lot about dolphins. Her friends had always wondered at how well she understood their language.

Then she heard voices in her helmet speaker. She saw the other scubaboards coming back.

"Sorry," Laura said. "We thought you were right behind us."

"It's OK," Ana replied.

"We couldn't catch up with the dolphins," said Daniel.

"But it looks as if one caught up with you," Laura noted.

Suddenly, the dolphin began to move its head up and down. It swam off a little ways. Then it stopped and looked back at the children.

"I think it wants us to come along," Ana said, putting her scubaboard in gear.

"Let's go!" Daniel said.

The children followed the dolphin. Soon they were met by a big group of dolphins. These dolphins swam around the scubaboards.

Ana pulled her scubaboard onto the sandy sea bottom. She waited for a dolphin to come close to her. Then she gently held on to its dorsal, or back, fin. She grinned as the dolphin pulled her along.

"Wow!" Daniel and Laura said together.

Suddenly, their fun was stopped by the sound of a low voice in their helmet speakers.

"Attention! All scubaboarders please return to the Starfish at once!"

"We'd better get back. Something important must have happened," said Daniel.

Sadly, the three children said goodbye to the dolphins. They pushed the HOME key on their boards and sped away.

They reached the Starfish in a short time. To get inside, they had to go through three ports, or doors, in a row. Each one led to a different entry room.

Ana, Daniel, and Laura left their scubaboards in the first room. They unzipped and took off their wetsuits in the second entry room. In the third room, they took quick showers and put on their indoor clothes.

When they stepped into the main hallway, people were hurrying everywhere. Daniel had been right. Something big was going on.

Chapter 2

Starfish on Alert!

As the children started to follow the crowd, Ana saw her mom. Dr. Ramirez hurried over to give Ana a hug. "Dr. Tan has called a meeting in the dining room," she said.

As they walked toward the dining room, Ana told her mom about the dolphins. "Do you feel a little better about the Starfish now that you have found dolphins?" Ana's mother asked.

"I think so," Ana replied. "But I still don't know if I can become a real Starfisher. Daniel called me a landlubber."

The dining room was crowded and noisy. Dr. Tan, the head scientist on the Starfish, called for attention.

"Our instruments on the sea floor show that an undersea earthquake will probably happen some time tomorrow. I want to have an earthquake drill today. Then the station will be on alert through tomorrow," Dr. Tan said.

Everyone started talking at once. Ana felt a little worried. *An earthquake!* she thought. *Would the Starfish be in danger?*

Ana hurried over to where Daniel and Laura were sitting. They were excited.

"What happens if there's an earthquake?" Ana asked. "What's an earthquake drill?"

"Don't worry, Ana. We'll show you what to do," Laura said. "We've had a couple of earthquakes while I've been on the Starfish. No one has been hurt. That's why we have the drills. And the Starfish is well built."

"I hope so," Daniel smiled. "But what if we got hit with a tsunami?"

"What's a tsunami?" Ana asked.

"Stop teasing her," Laura said to Daniel. "*Tsunami* means 'harbor wave' in Japanese. You say it like this: tsoo NAH mee. An undersea earthquake can start a tsunami. The wave travels very fast. It's not that noticeable out in the ocean. But when it gets close to land, it slows and grows. Then it becomes a tall, giant wave that can wash away everything on a coast."

"A tsunami wouldn't be a problem down here on the Starfish," Daniel explained. "Besides, we can put up special screens around the Starfish and around our underwater farms. The screens have lots of holes in them. Strong water currents are slowed down when they pass through the holes."

"Come on, Ana," Laura said, "I'll show you what to do for the drill."

Chapter 3

Rumbles and Shakes

That afternoon, the Starfishers went through the earthquake drill twice. Ana worked with her mother, who wore a headset so she could talk to the other scientists. They had to strap themselves into chairs attached to the floor. Then they were told how to look for any signs of damage along the outside wall. Later, they worked with a team that practiced putting up and taking down one of the screens around the farms outside the Starfish.

Finally, it was time for dinner.

"I'm starving," Laura said, when she met
Ana outside the dining room. "I wonder what's
for dinner?"

"Tacos," Daniel said, reading a menu posted
on the wall. It was dated October 25, 2053.

"They're probably seaweed tacos," he added.

The three children sat down at one of the tables.

"How did the drill go?" Laura asked Ana.

"Great!" Ana replied. "My mom and I went to the big viewing window. A dolphin swam by while we were there. Then we helped Team 1 put up a screen in three minutes."

"She'll be a Starfisher yet," Daniel teased.

Suddenly, Ana felt the floor shake. It moved up and down, then sideways. She heard the crash of dishes falling. Many people gasped. A few of the younger children started to cry. Daniel stood up, but he had trouble staying on his feet.

"What's happening?!" Ana yelled.

"It's the earthquake!" Laura yelled back.

"But it wasn't supposed to happen until tomorrow!" Daniel said.

"ATTENTION!" Dr. Tan's voice said from the wall speaker. "Everyone to your places. This is not a drill!"

Chapter 4

Aftershock

Ana stumbled out of the dining room. She ran as best she could to her place by the wall. Her mother was already there.

Ana strapped herself into her chair. She and her mother studied the wall carefully.

Finally, the shaking stopped. After the rumble of the earthquake, the Starfish seemed very quiet.

Ana's mother saw one tiny crack by the ceiling, but no water was coming through. She called for a repair crew.

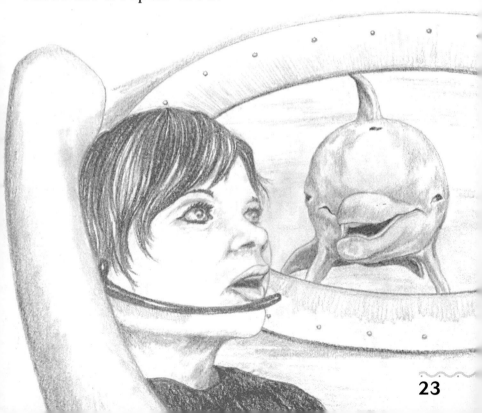

"Are you all right?" Dr. Ramirez asked Ana. They unstrapped themselves from their chairs and hugged each other.

"Yes, Mom," Ana replied. "Is the earthquake over?"

"We may feel a few aftershocks," her mom said. "They should not be nearly as strong as the main earthquake, though."

"We'd better rejoin our team to put up the screens," Dr. Ramirez added. "An earthquake that strong will make the water rough."

At the screen area, Ana and her mother worked quickly with their team. In minutes, all of the screens were up around the Starfish. Ana watched through the window. She could tell that the sea was becoming rougher.

Just then the wall speaker came on again.

"Everyone come to the main area at once," Dr. Tan's voice said. Ana and her mother rushed down the hall.

When they reached the dining room, almost all of the Starfishers were there. Daniel and Laura were each with their families. Many people looked dazed and tired.

"Quiet, please!" Dr. Tan said from the front of the room. The loud buzz of voices stopped.

"As you all know, the earthquake was unexpected. It happened nearly a day earlier than predicted," Dr. Tan said. "It was also stronger." Everyone nodded.

"I have just gotten a report that a large tsunami is building because of the quake. It's likely to head for the Hawaiian Islands," he said.

Someone cried, "Oh, no!"

"Don't worry," Dr. Tan said calmly. "The Worldwide Tsunami Monitoring System has already sent a warning. People on the main islands are moving to higher ground right now. Everyone should be safely out of the way by the time the tsunami reaches land."

"As for the Starfish," he continued, "our screens should take care of any problem we might have here."

Dr. Tan asked for reports about the slight damage caused by the earthquake. He was just about to close the meeting when his helper, Rob Gilman, came running into the room. He talked quickly to Dr. Tan.

"I have some bad news," Dr. Tan said to the group. "The smallest of the Hawaiian Islands has no higher ground for the people to move to. The wave is moving fast. There isn't time to find a boat big enough for the 300 people who live on the island."

The room was quiet. Ana thought about what Dr. Tan had said. The people on that island were in danger. She thought about the tsunami washing them into the ocean. She stared at the map on the wall. Wasn't there anything the Starfishers could do to help?

Chapter 5

A Rescue Is Planned

Everyone in the room seemed to feel the same way Ana did. From around the room came the question, "What can we do to help?"

"Tell me your ideas," Dr. Tan said.

"What about taking some of our screens to them?" a man asked.

"How would we get them there?" Dr. Tan asked.

"We could use the scubaboards to tow them. They're very fast," a woman said.

"That might work," Dr. Tan agreed. "But the screens were made for undersea use. They couldn't stop a wave that big at the surface. They might only slow it down a little."

"We could use the scubaboards to rescue the people," a boy said, raising his hand.

"Each board only holds three people at most," Dr. Tan said. "We wouldn't have time."

"What about our big transport?" a woman asked. "That holds almost 300 people. It's faster than the scubaboards."

"We could do that," Dr. Tan replied. "Could we get the transport ready to go right away?" The transport crew all nodded. "We could tell everyone on the island to be on the beach ready to go," he went on.

"Do you think we could beat the wave?" some people spoke.

"It would be very close," said Dr. Tan. "I wish there was a way to direct some of the water away from the island for just a few minutes."

"Let's take the screens and the transport," Daniel said. "We can tow the screens with the scubaboards. Maybe the screens will work."

"The chances of them working well enough are not good," Dr. Tan disagreed.

While everyone talked, Ana had been thinking hard. How could the water be directed to one side as well as slowed down? Then she recalled watching the dolphins.

"I have an idea," she said, raising her hand. Everyone turned to stare.

"Go ahead, Ana," Dr. Tan said kindly.

"What if we bent the top of each screen so that it was like the shape of a dolphin's fin," Ana suggested. "A dolphin's fins cut through and move water to one side. They also help the dolphin slow down."

The room was strangely quiet. Then Dr. Butler, the chief engineer, spoke. "That might work," she said. "The holes in the screens would slow the water. Then the bent top would redirect the water away. We have a machine that could easily bend those screens." As she talked, Dr. Butler drew a sketch.

Dr. Tan smiled. "I think we've got it!" he said. He pointed to Dr. Butler's picture. "We'd better get moving."

Everyone jumped out of their seats and ran from the room. Dr. Ramirez smiled proudly at Ana before they rushed off to help.

Chapter 6

Racing the Wave

Each team knew just what to do. One team raced to get the big transport ready to go. Another team ran to the scubaboards. A third team hurried to get the screens ready so the scubaboards could tow them. Still others dashed to the video equipment to send a message to the island. They told the people to gather on the beach as fast as possible.

"Mom, what are you going to do?" Ana asked.

"I'm going to help Dr. Jensen with the equipment that is tracking the tsunami," Dr. Ramirez replied. "You should go help Mrs. Minami get ready for the islanders when the transport returns."

"No, Mom, please," Ana said breathlessly.
"Please let me go with Laura and Daniel.
They'll be on their scubaboards."

"Ana, it's too dangerous," Dr. Ramirez said.
She stopped and looked at Ana. "A tsunami
can be deadly. The Starfishers are taking a
great risk trying this rescue."

"Mom, Laura already asked me to go. She
says I can make sure the screens are bent
correctly and put in the right place. It was my
idea," Ana cried.

"Let's talk to Dr. Tan," Ana's mother said.

They hurried to Dr. Tan. He listened to both Ana and her mother. Then he said, "It probably would be a good idea for Ana to go along. What if she rode in the transport instead of on a scubaboard? She'd be safer there."

"All right," Ana's mother said. She turned and hugged her daughter. "Just be careful," she said.

In less than an hour, the Starfishers were ready to go. The transport pulled away from the Starfish, followed by the scubaboards. The scubaboards pulled two big screens that had been bent over on one corner.

The transport was soon moving at top speed. It raced along the ocean bottom. From inside the transport, Ana watched the scubaboards following. *I wonder if we'll be in time,* she thought.

In a short time the transport neared the island. As it rose to the surface, the captain reported rough water.

Ana and several other people stood at the window as the top of the transport came out of the water. Ana could see the small island not far away. *It looks so peaceful,* she thought. Then she saw the people running to the beach.

Someone next to her shouted, "Look!" Ana turned to see what the woman was pointing to. In the distance, she could see a big bulge in the ocean. It was moving toward the island.

"The tsunami!" Ana cried.

Chapter 7

Tsunami!

As the transport moved toward the island, a strange thing started to happen. Suddenly, the ocean began to pull away from the island. The water ran down the beach uncovering the sand.

"What's happening?!" Ana asked.

"It's the tsunami," said the woman who stood next to her. "When the wave hits shallow water near land, it slows down. Then the wave begins to rise. It pulls the water away from the shore as it rises. Then the wave crests, or folds over on the top, and falls."

"We'd better hurry," Ana said. She turned and watched from the window as the scubaboards raced toward the island. They were towing the screens. Ana put a headset on so she could talk to Laura, Daniel, and the other scubaboard riders.

The scubaboards towed the screens to a spot in the water near the island and in front of the rising wave. Then they tried to raise them. They got them up, but they couldn't get them to stay together. The screens kept wobbling.

Ana was afraid they wouldn't be able to get the screens up in time to do any good. Then she spotted something moving in the water near the scubaboards.

"Those are dolphins!" she said into her headset. "Laura, show the dolphins what you want to do. They can help."

"Ana, you don't really think that will work do you?" Laura's voice sounded in Ana's ears.

"Yes, it will!" Ana cried.

Laura turned her scubaboard so that its nose pushed against the screen. At the same time, she raised one arm and moved her hand as if to say "Come on!" Then she made a pushing motion with her hands.

The dolphins swam around her scubaboard. Then they moved into a straight line in front of the screens. They placed their blunt noses up against the screens and began pushing. The screens moved together and locked into place.

The first part of the wave began to push up against the screens. The screens held steady while water began to run through the holes. At the top of the screens, the bent corners began to direct the water to one side.

"It's working!" Ana cried. She hopped up and down.

While the screens were being placed, the transport pulled up near the island beach. The door opened and a walkway came out to rest on the sand.

"Hurry!" yelled Dr. Tan to the people on the beach. One by one they ran into the transport.

Ana watched the screens. The wave grew bigger and taller behind them. Then one of the screens began to bend. The water was too strong. The screen was about to break!

"The screen is folding!" Ana yelled.

"Hurry! Get the rest of the people in!" Dr. Tan yelled.

The screens began to fold. The dolphins and the scubaboards had already gone under the water to safety.

The wave rose higher and higher. Ana could not even guess how high it was. It seemed to block out the sky. She saw the top begin to crest. It seemed to hang above the tiny island like a big monster.

Chapter 8

Just in Time

The door of the transport slammed shut. The last person from the island was on board!

"Get us out of here!" Dr. Tan yelled into his headset. "Get down on the floor, everybody! Hold on!" he yelled.

Ana fell to her knees. Then she spread herself out on the floor. She felt the transport go straight down like an elevator. The sudden drop knocked down anyone who was still standing.

As they sank quickly in the water, Ana heard a big roar from outside. The tsunami was hitting the island!

The rough water tossed the transport back and forth and up and down. But it kept moving deeper into the ocean. Finally, it was deep enough. The shaking stopped. Quickly, the transport began speeding across the ocean floor.

"Is the tsunami over?" Ana asked quietly.

"Almost," Dr. Tan told her. "The island has blocked part of it. The rest of it will hit the larger islands in just a few minutes. They should be OK, if everyone got away from the beach."

Dr. Tan shook Ana's hand. "Ana, you have been a great help," he said. "Your idea gave us those few extra minutes we needed. Now everyone from the island is safe."

Ana felt very tired. She just wanted to
find a quiet place to sit down. She walked
over to where everyone was seated.
She found a spot in the back from where
she could listen to Dr. Tan talk to the islanders.

He told them that they were on their way to
the Starfish. They would stay there for
a few days. When everything was quiet
back on shore again, the transport
would take them to one of the big
Hawaiian Islands.

As Ana listened, she
wondered if Laura and Daniel
were all right. She had
seen the scubaboards
sink and disappear into
the ocean before the
wave hit. However,
she could not be sure
if they had gotten
away safely. She
remembered how
the transport had
been tossed
around.

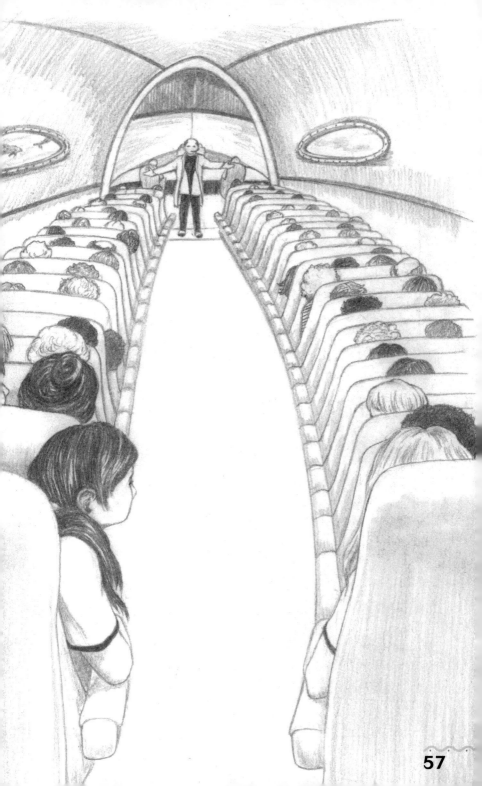

Chapter 9

Back Home

By the time the transport got back to the Starfish, Ana had fallen asleep. She was gently wakened by her mother. Dr. Ramirez had been the first Starfisher to meet the transport.

"Ana," she said. "Wake up. You're home."

At first, Ana didn't know where she was. When her mom said "home," she thought she was back on land in her old home. Then she remembered. She was back at the Starfish. She thought, *The Starfish is my home now*. She was surprised how good that idea felt.

Suddenly, Ana jumped up. "Mom," she said breathlessly. "Have you seen Daniel and Laura? Are they all right?" She tried to run.

"Hold on, Ana," her mom said, taking her hand. "Yes, they're fine."

"Let's go," Ana said, pulling on her mom's hand. They quickly walked to the dining room. The room was filled with people.

Ana stopped to look around. Then she saw Daniel and Laura seated at a table. They saw her, too, and waved.

"What happened to you when the tsunami hit?" Ana asked them as she hurried over.

"Wow!" Daniel said. "We got out of there just in time! It was a rough ride to the bottom."

"I almost fell off my scubaboard, but a dolphin pushed me back on. I don't think we could have made it without them. You were right about the dolphins, Ana," Laura added.

One of the video people came into the dining room. She called for quiet. Then she said, "We've had many calls from news reporters. They are asking if they can get a ride down here or if any of us can come to the mainland. They want to talk to anyone who was a part of the rescue."

Dr. Tan stood up. "I think we should send a small group to them," he said. "We're a little crowded down here now." Starfishers and islanders laughed along with Dr. Tan.

"I think that Daniel Fisher, Laura Marks, and Ana Ramirez should be a part of that group," Dr. Tan said. "Daniel and Laura were a big part of getting those screens in place. Ana's idea to bend those screens was what gave us a little extra time to get everyone on board the transport." Everyone clapped as Daniel, Laura, and Ana came to the front of the room.

After Ana talked to the reporters by video screen, she went to the rooms she and her mom shared. Her mom was already there.

"Exciting place, don't you think?" Dr. Ramirez asked.

"Oh, yes!" Ana said. "I don't think I've ever been so tired." She flopped down in a chair.

"There is one thing I know for sure," she added.

"What's that?" her mom asked.

"Daniel and Laura said I was a real Starfisher now. And I really feel like one!" Ana grinned.

GLOSSARY

alert (uh LURT) a warning of danger; a period of time until the danger has passed

coral (KOR ul) living animals in the ocean that form a hard reef or wall-like structure that is anchored to the ocean floor

crest (KREST) the line or surface along the top of anything, such as a wave

drill (drihl) group training and practice

earthquake (URTH kwayk) a shaking or sliding of the earth's surface caused by a sudden movement of rock far below

landlubber (LAND lub ur) someone who knows little about the sea

rescue (RES kyoo) to save someone or something from danger

scuba (SKOO buh) equipment worn by divers for breathing underwater

transport (TRANS port) a vehicle that is used to carry something from one place to another

wetsuit (WET soot) a rubber suit that fits tightly on the body and is used by divers to keep warm